LITTLE MISS APOCALYPSE

DANGER SLATER

ERASERHEAD PRESS
PORTLAND, OREGON

ERASERHEAD PRESS
833 SE Main St. #342
Portland, OR 97214

www.eraserheadpress.com

ISBN: 9781621053309
Copyright © 2023 by Danger Slater
Cover art copyright © 2023 by Attapol Kunya

Printed in the USA.

LITTLE MISS APOCALYPSE

CHAPTER ONE

Elizabeth Sturgis was ready to blossom like the rare and fragile orchid she always envisioned herself to be. There was nothing we could do to stop this from happening. Our young protagonist was growing up fast. Hidden in her was a power that had once gone unheralded, that we once underestimated, that we once ignored. But not for much longer. Armageddon loomed large before us, as inescapable as the senior prom that was coming up next week, because after Elizabeth Sturgis finally got her first kiss, the whole world would lay obliterated in her wake.

And while you and I went about our business as usual, completely unaware of our rapidly-approaching doom, Elizabeth Sturgis went about her business too, just as ignorant to her ultimate fate. She'd spent untold hours cloistered away in her bedroom, practicing her lip-locking techniques on a very befuddled couch pillow.

She ran her tongue along its ruffles, nibbled gently on its fabric folds. Not too forceful and not too wet, just like the video on YouTube instructed. She wanted to be ready for when the BIG DAY arrived. She just knew it was going to be absolutely…

…*perfect*.

So instead of picturing the planet engulfed in flames, charred human corpses littering the surface of the burning, lifeless Earth, this is how Elizabeth Sturgis imagined her first kiss would play out:

She'd be on the beach. And it would be after dark. And Trevor Sandstone would be there with her, and he would look so handsome because he ALWAYS looked handsome, even when he wasn't trying, and by this point in the story he'd be madly in love with her, just as she's long since been madly in love with him, and even though you're probably thinking there's no way in hell Trevor would be into her in real life, Elizabeth Sturgis would like to remind you that THIS IS HER GODDAMN FANTASY AND TREVOR SANDSTONE CAN BE MADLY IN LOVE WITH HER IF SHE WANTS, OKAY???

It's the summer after senior year, and she and Trevor will be walking barefoot in the cool, white sand while simultaneously gazing longingly into each other's eyes while simultaneously whispering sweet nothings into each other's ears while simultaneously having a candlelit dinner while he simultaneously gives her a box of chocolates and a dozen roses.

She'll cozy up next to him as he points out at the sea and says something profound about relationships and the sanctity of human connection amid the chaos of the vast and unknowable universe:

"Ya know, there are probably a buncha whales peeing and pooping in there right now."

Okay, so maybe what he says isn't very profound. Maybe it's better if he doesn't say anything at all. Maybe he just flexes his oiled-up biceps and smiles at her.

Elizabeth swoons. She's getting all horny for him, but not in the gross kind of way. Horny in the *romantic* kind of way. She looks up at the sky and it feels as if the moon and the stars were put there just for them. Those same stars dance with their reflections on the water below, and the ocean in front of them is lapping against the shoreline just like the ocean in her body is lapping against the backside of her underwear. Too graphic, you say? Too bad! Her love is an intrusive house guest who doesn't wait for her to open the door.

And then Trevor will lean in. And then Elizabeth will lean in too. And then their lips will touch. And his lips will be soft. Even softer than her pillow. Her skin will feel electric. Her toes and fingers will go numb. She'll be surging all over with...what were they called again? Hormones? It's hormones, right? Is that what she has been surging all over with lately? They were talking about it in health class earlier in the school year, but Elizabeth Sturgis wasn't paying attention to any of that crap because Mr. Belladonna was up in front of the room going:

Blah blah blah—menstruation—*blah blah*—body hair—*blah blah*—acne and mood swings and "making sure you take the proper precautionary measures to avoid the potential for swift and catastrophic nuclear annihilation"—*blah blah*.

It was BORING as SHIT.

That's why Elizabeth Sturgis wasn't listening. That's why she was staring at the moles on the back of Trevor Sandstone's neck instead, dreaming about beachside kisses and moonlit nights and all the babies they were going to make together after she graduated from college and got an important businessperson job at a fancy company. She was going to live in a mansion and make so much money that she'll be able to pay for her groceries with one of those black metal credit cards they only give to rich people and all the cashiers at Target will be SUPER impressed.

Yes, this was definitely LOVE she was feeling, not just some dumb schoolyard crush. This was the real friggin' deal. She felt it in her bones. She felt it like the air she breathed. Her love for Trevor Sandstone was SINCERE. And these mushy feelings were not just about DOING IT, even though DOING IT was a part of all this, sure. She was well aware that people in mature relationships had SEX all the time. Like three times a day, seven days a week, 365 days a year. This was normal. And given the opportunity, Elizabeth would gladly GO ALL THE WAY with Trevor Sandstone, and she'd do so with enthusiasm. Then it would be over and done with. She'd no longer be a virgin. She'd be an experienced and enlightened sexual being. No longer a girl, but a full-fledged woman. She'd learn all the positions for him too. Doggystyle. Froggystyle. Wormystyle. All the styles.

But this kind of love was more important than just DOING THE NASTY. Elizabeth Sturgis couldn't stress this enough. Trevor Sandstone was the captain of the basketball team and the most popular dude in school. He was traditionally attractive and when he smiled he got these little lines on either side of his mouth like a Hollywood leading man. Trevor could DO THE NASTY with anyone he wanted. He had his pick. But Elizabeth wanted him not just for his body, but also for his mind too. It's important to acknowledge that there's more to people than just their looks! She knew one day Trevor was going to grow old and wrinkly, and even though his genealogy and bone structure all but guaranteed he would age into a Jeff Goldblum-esque hot grandpa, the point was Elizabeth wasn't shallow and it was totally obvious to her that Trevor's dumb-ass girlfriend Helena Berkowitz didn't appreciate him for his brains like she would. Helena was only into him because he was popular and she was popular and popular people rarely stepped outside of their own ecosystems. Prom Queens dated Prom Kings. That's how it worked.

Man, Helena Berkowitz sucked hard even though she thought she was SO DAMN COOL because her uncle was the serial killer David Berkowitz aka the Son of Sam aka the .44 Caliber Killer.

"My uncle could totally murder your uncle," she'd always brag the other girls in the locker room. She was so stuck-up. She didn't deserve Trevor, even though she was probably right about the uncle thing. Elizabeth's uncle was a wimpy little nerd who couldn't murder anybody except for maybe himself because he was so stupid.

Before she was born Helena's dad wrote some crappy book about his famous serial killer brother and it sold four zillion copies and so her parents were rich. They even bought her a car.

But whatever. Fuck Helena right in her stupid eye socket. Let Trevor use that skanky ho for sex. She's basically just a human blow-up doll anyway. Elizabeth wasn't jealous in the slightest, although when she prayed to God at night, she'd always ask him to make Helena's tits get cancer and rot off.

For Elizabeth Sturgis, love was a rare and precious gem, reserved for Trevor Sandstone alone, the only one who could possibly find it buried deep within the mineshafts of her eager heart.

CHAPTER TWO

Elizabeth was eating beet salad at lunch and it stained her teeth red.

This goth kid who called himself Stevius Blaadfist came up to her and said "Whoa, you look pretty badass with your teeth all fucked up like that. You look EVIL, like you've been drinking BLOOD. Are you doing that on purpose because you believe in the power of the Dark Lord Satan?"

Elizabeth did NOT believe in the power of the Dark Lord Satan because that kind of stuff was for dorks, but Stevius looked so pathetically sincere as he stood there with his plastic lunch tray, a square slice of pizza and little box of 2% milk balanced on top. He smiled at her, revealing two fake fangs glued onto his incisors. Elizabeth didn't know him very well but they had a few classes together and he always looked as bored as she did so she figured he probably wasn't THAT bad for a goth-rock weirdo.

She ironically said, "Yes I do. Hail Satan or whatever." And she flashed him devil horns which Stevius thought was pretty funny because she had to think hard about how it was done. She was like a toddler trying to juggle.

"Cool. Well...I guess I'll catch ya later then, Bloodspilla," he said, returning the devil horns. "Enjoy the rest of your lunch."

"Later, Minion," Elizabeth replied giving him a sanguine grin.

CHAPTER THREE

"Elizabeth, can you come see me?"

That was what Mr. Belladonna said to her as she was floating through the hallway between classes like a ghost.

She could've probably thought of 8 million other things she'd rather do than talk to Mr. Belladonna, but he was standing there and staring at her like some kind of middle-aged mannequin so she didn't have much of a choice. His hair was getting thin and for some reason he put gel in it so it clumped up and looked even thinner. He wasn't ancient like most of the other teachers, but he was still pretty old. At least 30.

She went into Mr. Belladonna's classroom and sat down.

"Elizabeth," he said, "I was going over the results from last week's test..."

"And?"

"You did not do very well," he said.

"It's just one test. Who gives a flip? I was having a bad day. Is it illegal to have bad days now?"

"This isn't an isolated incident, Ms. Sturgis. You haven't passed a single test all year."

"Not for nothing, Mr. Belladonna, but health class is kinda a joke. Like math. Or English. When am I ever going to use this stuff in real life?"

He looked down at her exam sheet and then back up to her. "Elizabeth, judging from your answers here, you don't seem to know what a penis or a vagina even *are*, let alone what they're used for or how to practice any sort of sexual safety."

"Ew gross, Mr. B.," Elizabeth said. "Stop talking to me about penises and vaginas and S-E-X. That's perverted. I'm only 17.85 years old. You're super creepy for bringing this up around me. You're like a pedophile."

"Ms. Sturgis!"

"I'm sorry, Mr. Belladonna, but I don't need to worry about this kind of stuff, okay?"

"Oh? Why's that?"

"It's because I'm in love with someone and very soon they're going to realize they love me back and that's what really matters in life. Not a bunch of stupid tests. I mean, maybe it's not obvious to a creepy sex teacher like you, but love is the driving force behind almost all art and literature. I'm not some stupid little kid. I've seen tons of R-rated romantic comedies. Mostly stuff from the 80s, like the John Hughes stuff. And I even read a book once. Granted that book was *Winnie the Pooh*, but still, my point is, I know that once you and your soulmate fall in love everything else falls into place after that. You live happily ever after. It happens literally every time. So instead of bothering me, why don't you go read a book or rent a movie or whatever? All those idiot writers can't be wrong, can they Mr. B.?"

"Wait, you're...in love?" the teacher asked her, raising a skeptical eyebrow.

"Yeah, of course I am," she said. "Trevor Sandstone and I are on the verge of having a torrid affair. I'm telling you, when he and I kiss for the first time, it's going to feel just like fireworks..."

Mr. Belladonna almost choked to death on his coffee. His face turned purple before he finally swallowed. He shook his head pitifully.

"Oh honey," he said. "I'm sorry. I didn't mean to almost choke to death in front of you, but I can most certainly assure you that your feelings for Trevor only go one way."

"Wha—what are you saying, Mr. B.?" she innocently said.

Mr. Belladonna sighed. "I'm saying...Trevor isn't in love with you, and I'm 99.99% sure he never will be. He's the captain of the basketball team. He's super popular. He's funny and good-looking and charismatic. I hear he even got offered a contract to go model for American Apparel in LA but he turned it down so he could focus on his scholarship to Yale. Hell, even *I* want to be friends with him. You, on the other hand? You're the third-string benchwarmer on our school's competitive cheese-eating team. I'm not trying to hurt your feelings, but it would never work, Elizabeth. You're not even good enough to eat cheese at a varsity level."

"Ugh. What the hell do you know anyway?" Elizabeth scoffed at her teacher. "You're, like, a gagillion years old. If they made an 80s teen comedy out of your life it would be called *Sixteen HUNDRED Candles* and it would star you and Molly Methuselah Tree and the opening scene would take place during the Big Bang."

The teacher just shook his head. "Look, regardless of any of *that*, the stuff I'm trying to teach you is important, Ms. Sturgis. Personal health and sexual education. It's vital that you know and understand the changes your body is going through..."

Elizabeth sat there rolling her eyes over and over again, so much so that she got dizzy.

"OMG is that all?" she finally asked.

"Yeah, that's all," Mr. Belladonna replied.

And she got up and left.

CHAPTER FOUR

"Hey, Bloodspilla, wait up!" she heard a voice call out as she walked home from school.

She turned around and saw Stevius running to catch up to her. All the metal chains hanging off his bondage pants were going *clang clang clang* against his thighs as he skipped across the street. Skipping wasn't necessarily a very goth thing to do, but Stevius did it in the most goth-y way he could think of, which meant he skipped with BROODINESS and ENNUI. At least he was trying, thought Elizabeth. She decided to be nice and not make fun of him.

"Oh, Minion, it's you. What are you doing here?" she said. "Looking for human sacrifices or whatever?"

"Nah, nothing cool like that. I saw you by yourself and I just thought maybe you'd like someone to walk you home," he said.

"Of course I would like someone to walk me home..." she replied.

Stevius smiled.

"...except that person isn't you. It's Trevor Sandstone."

His smile dropped. "Yeah, I suppose that makes sense. Trevor is a pretty cool dude, for sure. I mean, I still hope he dies in a house fire and all that, but even I can admit that, objectively-speaking, he's the most beautiful man I've ever seen."

And as if on cue, Trevor and his crew rounded the corner in his Audi A5 Cabriolet. He was blasting some really cool new rap song from some up-and-coming artist that nobody knew about yet but everyone would be to be talking about in a few weeks. Helena Berkowitz was in the passenger seat and her hair was dancing perfectly in the wind, somehow never landing in front of her face. And his multicultural group of friends were in the back, including Darius Moore -the COOLEST black kid in school- and Annabel Lu -the COOLEST Asian girl in school.

"Look at how COOL and racially diverse they are," Elizabeth said. "Damn it, Stevius, why couldn't you be more ASIAN or something?"

"I'm actually half-Zapotec," he said.

"What the hell is that?"

"Indigenous Mexican," he replied. "From the Oaxaca region, if you want to get specific. Not for nothin' but I guess that makes me the COOLEST Zapotec person in our school by default, right?"

"What about Hector Moreno? Is he Zapotec?"

"Shit. I forgot about him."

Trevor leaned out his car window as he sped by and launched a full milkshake at the two of them. "Bombs away, nerds!" he yelled. The cup missed Elizabeth but hit Stevius on the side of the head. It exploded, drenching the unsuspecting boy from head to toe in viscous pink slime.

The popular kids drove away, laughing.

"OMG, I think Trevor accidentally dropped his milkshake on you," Elizabeth said. "That cup was very full. He must have been thirsty. Perhaps I should buy him a new one."

Stevius ran his index finger along his cheek and then put it in his mouth.

"Strawberry," he said. "I hate strawberries."

CHAPTER FIVE

Later that night, Elizabeth was laying in bed, scrolling through Instagram on her phone.

She clicked over to Helena Berkowitz's profile and started 'liking' and then 'unliking' all of the photographs Helena and Trevor were in together. Like this picture of the two of them sharing a ridiculously giant cotton candy as some sort of dumbass carnival? LIKE/UNLIKED! Or this one of them sitting on the dock at Gunner Bathory's lake house, laughing over some HILARIOUS thing that's happening somewhere off-camera? LIKE/UNLIKED! Or how about this one of them kissing??????? Ugh, that's so fuckin' gross!

LIKE/UNLIKED/LIKE/UNLIKED/LIKE/UNLIKED!

She navigated over to Trevor's Twitter feed and read his last status update:

TOTALLY MILKSHAKED SOME GOTH NERD TODAY. HE LOOKED LIKE A IDIOT, ALL MILKSHAKEY AN' SHIT. WHAT A DWEEBY LI'L BITCH!

In the past 30 minutes, his post had been retweeted over 185 times. So Elizabeth clicked retweet too. She didn't want to be left out.

A chat window then popped up from someone named Stephen Finkelstein.

"Hey Elizabeth," the text appeared.

"Um...who is this?" Elizabeth replied.

"It's Stevius. You know, from school?"

"Oh right. I forgot you had an actual name."

"Yeah, this dumb messaging app won't let me change it. But Stephen Finkelstein is my fake normie name. It was given to me when I was born, thrust into this world of PAIN. Stevius is my *real* name. It's who I am ON THE INSIDE."

"Whatever that means lol," Elizabeth typed. "So why are you bothering me, you DWEEBY LI'L BITCH?"

"Um...well...listen, I was thinking…I know proms are totally boring and they suck and only bourgeois assholes go to them and I would NEVER be caught dead at one - but I kinda want to go anyway because I recognize that at some point in the future I might not be so full of angst and if I skip out on this shared societal milestone, I might regret it later, ya know? So I was wondering if you'd want to be my date?"

"Are you KIDDING me? Lololololololol,"

Elizabeth said. "Look, Stevius, you're okay for a goth kid, but I'm 99.99% sure Trevor is going to ask me any day now, so thanks but no thanks. I think I'm going to hold out and wait for him."

A minute or two passed before Stevius finally typed his response:

"Oh. Okay then. I guess I'll see you at school tomorrow?"

"Whatever," she replied before closing out the window.

She then clicked back over to Trevor's Instagram. There was a picture of him at a basketball game, all covered in sweat. He was dribbling the ball and looking determinedly ahead. In the background of the photo, among the out-of-focus throngs that filled the stands, sandwiched in the center of all those people, was a blur in particular that Elizabeth thought might've been her. She tried to tag herself but the stupid app would let her. Oh well.

She tagged herself as Trevor's basketball instead.

CHAPTER SIX

The next day at lunch Elizabeth was eating a hard-boiled egg and it made her breath smell like someone farted in her mouth but it was healthy and it tasted alright so why don't you shut the fuck up about her bad breath already, okay?

Trevor was at a table on the other side of the room, surrounded by his friends. He turned his chair backward and sat confidently with his legs spread wide open. He didn't care about industrial design or ergonomics. His hat was turned backward too. He didn't care about sun glare either.

She knew she had to do something to get his attention.

"Hey, Finkelstein!" Elizabeth said to Stevius who was sitting at a nearby table all by himself, eating a beet salad like he had seen her do the day before.

"Huh?" he looked up.

"Hey," she got up and sat down next to him. "Stop

23

eating disgusting salad for a second. Your face looks like it's on its period. I need your help."

"Why would I help you with anything? You turned me down for the prom yesterday and called me a dweeby li'l bitch, remember?"

"Jeeeeeezus, could you stop making this all about yourself for, like, five friggn' seconds? I never said you were a dweeby li'l bitch. You must've misread what I typed because those albino contacts you wear are making you blind."

He sat back in his chair, lapsing into silence.

"C'mon, Minion. I'm sorry, alright? I didn't mean it. Please, I can't do this without you."

"Fine, I'll help you," he eventually conceded. "But only under one condition. Since you're not gonna go with me, you're gonna have to help me score a date to prom with someone else instead. It's only fair. Tit for tat, or whatever that saying is."

"OH MY GAWD, FINKELSTEIN, you're making my life a living hell..." she dramatically groaned before her glance drifted its way over to Trevor who was now doling out wedgies, one-by-one, to a line of complacent and grateful nerds. He looked so big and strong bullying those kids that Elizabeth almost peed herself from horniness. "Okay fine. Whatever. Which one of these SKANKY-ASS SKANKS were you thinking about asking?"

"Well if you're so certain that Trevor and you are gonna go together, then that means Helena Berkowitz won't have a date, so I was thinking..."

"OMG, HELENA BERKOWITZ, ARE YOU

SERIOUS RIGHT NOW?!? SHE'S THE BIGGEST SLUT IN THE HISTORY OF SLUTDOM!"

"That's not true," said Stevius. "You just don't like her because she's mean to you. She's a 10. And her uncle is the Son of Sam. That's super goth-y! I wonder if she has bones in her closet. Ya know, like souvenirs from him?"

"Well my uncle worked at *Home Depot* but you don't hear me bragging all over creation about his closet full of hammers," Elizabeth mumbled.

"Liz...are you...jealous?"

"Don't be ridiculous," she scoffed. "I don't care what you do. You can have sex with The BTK Killer's niece and The Night Stalker's niece and every other serial killer's niece if you want. You can have sex with them all in one big blood orgy. You're being stupid."

"Whatever," he said, sinking his glued on fangs into another beet.

Her gaze founds its way to Trevor once again.

"Okay fine, it's a deal," she finally said. "We'll help each other get prom dates if you promise to stop eating that gross food like that. Now c'mon. I have an idea."

CHAPTER SEVEN

Elizabeth dragged Stevius out of the lunchroom and they make their way down the hall. They hid from the hall monitor by ducking behind some lockers.

"How are we gonna get around him?" asked Stevius.

Elizabeth made a little chirpy bird sound. When the hall monitor went to investigate, she struck him in the head with an American History textbook and knocked him unconscious.

"Oh my god, that was fucked up!" Stevius shouted. "Is he going to be okay? We should call an ambulance. You can't mess around with head injuries like that."

"Shut up and c'mon," she whispered as she pulled her new friend into the auditorium.

The room was empty. Only a few lights were on, mostly directed towards the stage. The two of them ran up the stairs and looked out at the vacant audience.

"Oh yes," Elizabeth said. "The lighting up here is perfect. This is definitely the spot."

"The spot for what?" asked Stevius. There was a shitty cutout castle set half-painted behind them. He picked up a script laying there. *Love's Labour's Lost* it was called. He read a few lines:

"*Prepare, madam, prepare!*
Arm, wenches, arm! Encounters mounted are
Against your peace. Love doth approach disguis'd
Armed in arguments, you'll be surpris'd."

"Stop saying nonsense words," she said as she took her shirt off.

"Whoa, what the heck is going on? Are we going to lose our virginities to one another for practice? Because I'll be honest with you, this is EXACTLY how I always pictured it."

"Ew, gross! NO, you freak!" she said as she tossed Stevius her cellphone. "You're going to take sexy pictures of me and we're going to send them to Trevor. To seduce him."

"Oh," Stevius said. "Yeah, I was just kidding about the virginity thing anyway. I'm not a virgin. I wouldn't want my coven to sacrifice me to Satan, which is what we do to virgins when we find them, by the way. I bang chicks all the time. I bang so many chicks it makes me want to vomit. They call me Cassanova. Or maybe it's Bossanova? Either way, I'm VERY experienced when it comes to sexual intercourse and I'm certainly NOT getting an erection right now because that would be an amateur move..."

Elizabeth had taken off her pants and was in her underwear now.

Stevius held up her phone and went to take a picture.

"No, you idiot," she said. "I'm not posing sexily. I'm just standing here like a fat normal person. We need to get a good angle."

"So pose sexily then."

She awkwardly put her leg up on a chair and curled her arm under her chin, like that statue, The Thinker.

"Nope," he said. "You look like you're taking a dump."

"I've got it," she replied.

She took off her underwear and bent over and grabbed a fistful of asscheek in each hand. She pulled her butt apart so that her asshole was blinking at Stevius like a Cyclops eye. He stood there, staring at it, his mouth agape.

"What are you doing, dummy? Take a picture of my butthole so I can send it to Trevor."

Stevius held up the camera.

"No, get closer," Elizabeth instructed him. "There's too much background crap."

"What about ambiance?" Stevius said.

"This isn't about ambiance," she replied. "This is about eroticism. Now get in there."

Stevius took a few steps and held up the camera again.

"Closer!" she said. "Hurry up, there's a draft in here. It's like this whole goddamn school is in Antarctica."

Stevius moved even closer. He was just a few inches from her bare butt, the camera pointed directly at her blushing brown eye. His heart raced. He skin got clammy. This was the perfect moment, he thought. He had to make a move. He leaned in and started licking her ass out.

"Stevius?" she said, confusedly, and yet she didn't flinch or pull away. In fact -AND DON'T YOU *DARE* TELL ANYONE ABOUT THIS- but she felt something within herself suddenly wake up. Something was emanating from deep inside of her body. A quiver. A rumble. A squishy, slippery sensation unlike any she'd ever felt before. It started at her abdomen and traveled throughout all of her limbs before finding its home between her hips.

Before she knew what was happening exhaust started leaking out from between her legs, thick plumes of gray smoke billowing up to the ceiling of the auditorium so that it hung over the two of them like a cloud. It rolled, folded, swelled and swirled. In her head all she could hear was the sound of air raid sirens suddenly going off, the electronic wail warning her that something terrible was about to happen. The cloud above them was slowly building towards an apogee, like a dark sky on the verge of rain. But before the thunder could clap a voice interrupted them:

"JESUS CHRIST WHAT IS HAPPENING HERE?!" it yelled out.

Stevius jerked his face away from Elizabeth's butt and she quickly pulled up her trousers. The smoke dissipated to reveal Mr. Belladonna standing in the back of the room, horrified.

CHAPTER EIGHT

Elizabeth Sturgis and Stevius Blaadfist sat in detention, which was complete bullshit because nowhere in the district charter did it say you couldn't take sexy pictures on school grounds. Even the asshole licking incident was pretty benign, as far as asshole licking goes. Mr. Belladonna was such a prude. Mr. Belladonna probably showered with all his clothes on. Mr. Belladonna was probably born wearing a three-piece business suit and when he popped out of his mother, he looked at his watch and was all like 'Gee Willikers, wouldja look at the time! I'm late for work! Toodle-loo!'

The most confusing part of this entire situation was the pillars of smoke that had poured out of her... ~~vagina~~...her *CUPCAKE*. What the heck was that all about? She even swore she heard a countdown begin, the voice of a computer echoing against the backside of her ears. It was frightening, but admittedly, a little exciting too. Did they cover this kind of stuff in health class or not? She couldn't remember. The human body truly was a mystery.

Either way, both her and Stevius were now in detention and it was complete bullcrap!

This whole dumb situation probably would've been a lot more manageable if it had played out just like it did in *The Breakfast Club.* How come no one ever tried to lick Ally Sheedy's butthole in that movie? So unrealistic. No one tried to lick her butthole in *Short Circuit* either. Elizabeth wondered what kind of hack was writing these things? Getting your ass licked out is OBVIOUSLY a normal part of the modern teenage experience.

Mr. Belladonna sat in the front of the classroom like a big fat turd, turding up the joint.

"You gotta help me now," Stevius whispered to Elizabeth.

"Help you what?" Elizabeth said.

"Help me seduce Helena," he replied.

"EWW! NO WAY!" she shouted.

"Shhhhhh," Mr. Belladonna shot them both a reprimanding look before returning his gaze to the newspaper on his desk.

"I'm not helping you," Elizabeth said, lowering her voice again. "That picture you took is totally blurry and unusable. Not to mention the whole butt-eating thing. So weird. Plus, your hair is so long you're almost a girl yourself. And sorry, but I'm not a lesbian."

"Hey, we had an agreement," Stevius said. "You help me and I help you. It's exactly the same as the plot of that movie *Whatever It Takes*."

"WHAT THE HELL? THAT'S A 90s TEEN COMEDY!" a horrified Elizabeth Sturgis cried out. "HAVEN'T YOU BEEN PAYING ATTENTION? I ONLY LIKE TO REFERENCE 80s MOVIES!"

"Ms. Sturgis!" Mr. Belladonna scolded her again.

"I'm sorry, Mr. B. but 90s teen comedies are the literal *WORST*. They're so derivative of the far superior films that came the decade before!"

"I hate to burst your bubble kiddo, but even though principal filming took place in 1999, *Whatever It Takes* didn't receive a theatrical release until the year 2000, therefore invaliding your entire argument," her teacher corrected her. "Perhaps you should be referencing something that actually came out in the 90s, Ms. Sturgis, like *10 Things I Hate About You*."

"That's a good movie," Stevius said. "It's actually based off *The Taming of the Shrew* by Shakespeare, so it's derivative by design."

"YOU'RE based off Shakespeare," Elizabeth smugly replied.

"Do you even know who Shakespeare is?" Stevius asked.

"Of course I do," Elizabeth said. "He wrote that Claire Danes/Leonardo DiCaprio movie. *Titanic*, or whatever it was called."

"Look, are you going hold up your end of the bargain or not?" he said.

"Fine, fine, I'll help," Elizabeth replied. "But it doesn't matter how close we get, I'm not going to put my tongue in your asshole, okay?"

CHAPTER NINE

Elizabeth Sturgis looked at the pentagram arranged out of stones on the ground.

Stevius had lead her into the woods. He said that most things involving devil worship usually happened in the woods. When you're in the woods you can commune more easily with the spirits or whatever, he told her. He even called the camp they were at Camp Evil, which wasn't a very clever name, but Elizabeth decided not to say anything about it because she didn't want to hurt his feelings.

"Camp Evil, are you fucking serious right now?" she mocked him.

Oh, maybe Elizabeth *did* say something about it.

"Laugh all you want, but you'll see. I'm going to perform a satanic ritual in order to make myself irresistible to Helena," he said.

"Why do you need me here for this anyway?" asked Elizabeth. "You know I don't really believe in any of this demonic shit, right?"

"I need your virgin blood," he said. "To perform the spell."

"You want my blood?"

"Not all of it. Just a little bit should work. A couple of squirts, tops."

"Ugh, whatever, FINE!" She rolled her eyes at him and produced a small vial of her blood from her pants pocket. "You're lucky I just happened to have this on me."

Stevius took it from her and placed it along with a stuffed teddy bear at the center of the pentagram.

"Whoa, whoa, whoa! What are you going to do with that?" said Elizabeth, pointing to the perpetually happy-faced bear.

"According to the satanic message boards I frequent, I'm supposed to sacrifice an animal while I recite the incantation. But I don't want to hurt an *actual* animal because I'm vegan."

"What are you talking about? You're not a vegan."

"I sure am," he said. "Except for the leather in my bondage pants, which I bought before I went cruelty-free. Oh, and I sometimes put milk in my cereal, which doesn't count either because, c'mon, who the hell is gonna eat dry cereal? And I eat fish too, on occasion. And chicken. And hot dogs. And veal. Okay, basically I eat whatever my parents cook for dinner. But other than that, I'm a vegan. So I'm going to sacrifice this stuffed animal instead of a live one. I think the Dark

Lord will understand that I have ethical convictions and he'd probably respect me for sticking to them."

"Where did you even get that ratty-looking thing? Is it yours?"

"JESUS GOD NO!" Stevius shouted. "I'd never harm Mr. Teddles! No, this ugly fucking bear belongs to my dumb kid sister."

"So what happens now?" Elizabeth Sturgis was growing increasingly more bored with how boring the woods were. Like, you've seen one tree, you've seen them all…

"Now I'm going to recite an incantation and become all-powerful and then use the influence of Beelzebub to hypnotize Helena into being my slave. Or something along those lines."

"So ridiculous. I'm pretty sure this is illegal. Not that I think it matters, because if this works I will literally kiss a worm," she said.

"Well you better pucker up because I'm about to blow your friggin' little mind."

Elizabeth stepped back and gave Stevius a doubtful look which he completely ignored because what the fuck does Elizabeth know about the occult anyway?

He stood at the edge of the pentagram and raised his skinny arms to the sky.

"*Abe due damballa, give me the power I beg of you*
Abe due damballa, give me the power I beg of you
Abe due damballa, give me the power I beg of you
Abe due damballa, give me the power I BEG OF YOU!"

"OMG," Elizabeth burst out laughing, "Are you

quoting Chucky's voodoo spell from those stupid *Child's Play* movies?"

"First off, those movies aren't stupid, they're cool," said Stevius. "Secondly, where else am I supposed to find a ritualistic satanic prayer?"

"I dunno. A library, maybe?"

"What am I, a mega-dork? I'm not going into a library," he said. "Anyway, shut-up and look at the sky. It's getting sinister out here. My prayer is totally working..."

And Stevius was right. A dark, ethereal storm cloud rolled in, tumultuous, unsettling, churning like liquid. The Earth shook and the ground grew unsteady, swelling up beneath them like a giant blister. Elizabeth almost lost her balance but managed to brace herself against a nearby stump.

"It's working!" cried Stevius. "I can't believe it! It's actually working!"

A lightning bolt came tumbling down from the heavens, striking the dirt just a few feet in front of them. The soil split open and a huge pillar of volcanic hellfire blasted upward. All these cheap, wispy trails of cartoonish-looking electricity zapped their way across Stevius's body as he stood there in front of the flames and convulsed, a smile on his face amid the chaos.

"I am so powerful!" he cried out. "I feel like a GOD!"

And then there was a flash. And when Elizabeth's eyes readjusted she saw that the sky had returned to normal and the hellfire was gone and Stevius Blaadfist was gone too, or at least he was gone in the form that we knew him before because now he had been replaced by a two-foot tall stuffed doll version of himself.

"Uh...hmm...I don't think I did this right..." he said as he took a glance down to his now-plastic hands. He opened and closed his stiff fingers, rubbed his toy arms across his cotton-bloated belly. He was soft in the middle, filled with fluff and sewn together along his spine, but his face and appendages were made out of painted rubber. He looked kinda like a gothic Cabbage Patch Kid.

"Dummy, you sacrificed a stuffed bear instead of a real animal while referencing a movie about a man whose soul gets trapped in a doll. What did you expect to happen?"

"Yeah? Well if you're so smart then why didn't you say something five minutes ago Little Miss I-Know-Everything-After-The-Fucking-Fact?"

Elizabeth picked him up and squeezed him and a little plastic bulb somewhere inside of him went *squeak*.

"Stop it!" he said, wiggling out of her grasp. "This is terrible. Helena Berkowitz isn't going to want to go to the prom with a stuffed doll version of me."

Elizabeth shrugged and said, "In all fairness, Helena Berkowitz wasn't going to want to go to the prom with the regular version of you either."

CHAPTER TEN

That night Elizabeth borrowed her mother's Carolla but she didn't ask for permission because her mother would've said NO and ARE YOU CRAZY? and YOU DON'T EVEN HAVE A LICENSE. But what difference did any of THAT make when you've got a hot date with the hottest person in school? And even though Elizabeth didn't *actually* have a hot date with the hottest person in school, she did see *License to Drive* starring both Corey Haim AND Corey Feldman (aka "The Coreys") and the whole plot of that movie revolved around driving around without a license and everything turned out okay for them in the end so her mother was just being a stupid idiot who never watched movies and didn't know shit about being a teenager.

Anyway, she drove her mother's car to Trevor's street. She made sure to drive it carefully because she didn't want to get a ticket or anything like that. Her mom would ground her for sure if she knew what she was up to.

She pulled up to the curb a few houses down from Trevor's place. She could see his silhouette in his first-story bedroom window, the light behind him outlining his muscly body like a shadow puppet.

The car idled. Elizabeth could feel the vibrations from the engine travel from the gas pedal, up her leg, to her hips. Her pelvis shimmied and shook like she was sitting on a washing machine. And she dared not blink as she watched the dark figure of Trevor Sandstone do the kind of things a guy like Trevor Sandstone did at night: He curled dumbbells so that his biceps bulged out even further. He chugged cans of Mountain Dew as practice for when he was going to chug Coors Lights in college. He logged on his computer to cyberbully other kids at school in weirdly homoerotic ways, saying things like, "Hey Finkelstein, how come you weren't looking at my beautiful dick in the locker room, you queer?"

She thought about what it would be like to be in his room with him. Maybe blending in with the clutter in his closet like ET did in *ET: The Extraterrestrial.* Maybe she could even be eating Reese's Pieces like that gross-ass alien did in that movie. Reese's Pieces were FUCKING DELICIOUS!

And the car vibrated, soft and rhythmic. And Elizabeth Sturgis vibrated soft and rhythmic too, the sensation echoing back from somewhere deep inside her. Her body was lit up like a school of electric eel, and the front of her pants began to get very hot. Right between her legs. Radiating outward from the inside of her private parts. From inside of her *CUPCAKE*. It was intense, but it wasn't without its pleasures. So she leaned into it, letting the feeling overtake her. She could feel her body getting hotter and hotter. So hot, in fact, that smoke began pouring out of her crotch once again, like her legs were the gaping jaws of a dragon. The whole car quickly filled up with her exhaust. She heard alarms honking, warning bells ringing, a countdown from somewhere in her pelvis commenced:

"*T-minus 10 seconds to ignition...*" a computerized voice said through a loudspeaker inside her.

She rolled down the windows and wafted the smoke away and was able to see a second shadow in Trevor's room now. A female shadow. She had a droopy butt and flat-pancake boobs and curly hair like a bunch of Amazonian vines were growing out of her head.

"*7 seconds...*"

WHO THE HELL IS THAT?! It definitely wasn't Helena. Helena had a hot body that was unmistakable even though she was the skankiest skank to ever show up to dinner on Skanksgiving.

"*4 seconds...*"

More smoke. Almost too thick to breathe. For Elizabeth Sturgis, it felt like the whole world had caught on fire. Even behind her eyes seemed to flicker with orange light.

Trevor and this womanly figure danced.

"*3 seconds...*"

They leaned in like they were kissing.

"*2 seconds...*"

He slowly pushed her head down to his own crotch.

"*1 secon—*"

Elizabeth couldn't take it anymore. Who the frick was this ho-bag getting freaky with her ONE TRUE LOVE? She threw the car in drive and stepped on the gas.

"*Launch sequence aborted,*" the robotic voice inside of her said as her mother's car speed down the street, jumped the curb, and headed straight into the wall of Trevor's bedroom. His entire house shook as the Toyota Carolla smashed through the building's flimsy façade. Elizabeth couldn't believe how easy it was to drive a car through the wall of a house. What do they make houses out of in this crappy town anyway? Paper maché?

Trevor and his floozy were flung backward from the impact. Trevor tumbled over his bed and landed on his butt, but the girl struck the far wall with such force that her head exploded like a cantaloupe. Elizabeth experienced a moment of pure horror. Did she accidentally just murder some skanky cantaloupe-headed ho? I mean, it's pretty strange that this girl's head was an ACTUAL, LITERAL cantaloupe with googly eyes glued on and a hole cut into it for a mouth, wasn't it? What's the deal here?

She looked at the body and on closer inspection was relieved to see that this girl wasn't a girl at all, but rather, an improvised sex doll that Trevor had built out of some junk he'd found laying around the house. Her hair was simply a wig made out of an old mop and her body was constructed from his dead grandmother's muumuu, stuffed full with dirty socks until it took on a crude feminine shape. There was an open lubed-up Gatorade bottle where it's lady bits should be.

Trevor was into some weird perverted shit. Elizabeth wanted to reference an 80s movie here, but oddly enough, she couldn't remember one where a situation quite like this happened before.

The last bits of smoke cleared from her crotch as the shock of the impact wore off. Trevor poked his head up from the side of the bed and glared at Elizabeth in the driver's seat of the car. His big beautiful brown eyes met hers.

"What the FUCK are you doing, you crazy cunt?!" he screamed.

OMG he talked to her!

CHAPTER ELEVEN

Elizabeth's mother was livid, of course. She'd clearly forgotten what it was like to be in love. All she cared about was her stupid broken car and the $40,000 worth of structural damage Elizabeth had caused to The Sandstones' house. Like she couldn't just pick up a few extra hours at work and pay for it. Why did she have to act like every little dollar was worth a thousand dollars?

They drove back from the police station in silence, and when they got home her mother told her to go to her room and not come out.

"I can't come out? What if the house is on fire?"

"Okay, if the house is on fire you can come out."

"And what about school?"

"Obviously you still have to go to school, Elizabeth. Don't be dense. I'm grounding you, not giving you a vacation."

"Grounding me? Are you fuckin' serious right now mom? The prom is in a few days."

"You drove my car into a boy's bedroom. You could've killed him."

"No I couldn't! He jumped out of the way!"

"And what if he didn't?" she said. "What if you ran him over?"

Elizabeth's face lit up. "And then I had to take care of him and nurse him back to health like in my favorite romantic comedy *Misery*?"

Her mother sighed in exasperation. For a moment Elizabeth considered asking her about the smoke and the alarms that had been emanating from out of her body, but quickly brushed the idea off. It was an embarrassing personal problem, surely. Like flatulence or biting your nails or booger-eating or hair-eating. If her mom didn't understand what would compel her to drive a car full-speed into a cute boy's house, what could she possibly understand about biology?

"Do you have any idea how difficult it is to be a single parent?" her mother said.

"Jee-zus mom, please don't start in on me with this guilt trip again. So dad got eaten alive by sharks at SeaWorld after slipping on a banana peel and falling into an open tank? So what? It could happen to anyone if they're clumsy enough. I was there, I saw it happen with my own two eyes, and yet you don't hear me using it to make excuses."

"Are you serious?" she said. "Literally ALL you do is make excuses, Elizabeth."

"But that's only because everyone is in my way all the time! Everyone treats me like I'm some kinda bald-headed baby. I'm not a little kid anymore!"

"No, you're *not* a little kid anymore," her mother concurred. "And that's why you're not going to prom, dear. You need to learn there are consequences for your actions. You can't just barrel your way through life and expect everything to work out perfectly like it does in the movies."

"But life imitates art, you dumb hag. Haven't you ever heard that saying before? Why would people say it if it wasn't true? Is the world full of liars?"

"You're lucky you're still under 18 or else you'd be in prison right now."

"I AM in a prison. A prison of your BULLSHIT RULES."

"I'm sorry, Elizabeth but that's final. No prom."

"GOD, YOU'RE BEING SUCH A BITCH ABOUT THIS," Elizabeth screamed into her mother's face before stomping through the living room and up the stairs. "I HATE YOUR STUPID GUTS! I WISH YOU WERE THE ONE THAT GOT EATEN ALIVE BY SHARKS! I WISH EVERYONE WOULD JUST SHUT UP AND GET EATEN ALIVE BY SHARKS!"

CHAPTER TWELVE

The next day in health class Mr. Belladonna was talking about penises and vaginas AGAIN. It was like he was OBSESSED with those things. If somebody wrote a biography about Mr. Belladonna it would just be the words 'penis' and 'vagina' over and over again, 60,000 times. And when Elizabeth Sturgis got bored listening to him, which she invariably did because Mr. Belladonna was a boring cow, she drew a doodle of Trevor Sandstone and it looked like this:

Hey, don't you dare fucking sit there and judge her crappy drawing, okay? You don't write for the New York Times Arts & Culture section, do you? Well then shut the hell up.

Anyway, Mr. Belladonna was prattling on and on about vas deferens and vuvlas and whatnot when the bell rang. Trevor stood up and Elizabeth quickly shoved her drawing in her mouth so he wouldn't see it.

Normally, Trevor would rush out of the room so he could go finger Annabel Lu in the backseat of his Audi like he did every day after health class, but instead, on this day, he turned around and faced her.

He said: "Hey, um, Lisa?"

"Mah name eth Elwizabeff," she said through a mouthful of paper.

"What?"

She swallowed the drawing.

"My name is Elizabeth," she said. "But you can call me Lisa if you want. You can call me Lezzybeth or Elizabarf or Lizardbutt whatever other demeaning nicknames you can come up with. I honestly don't mind."

"Look, you're not going to tell anyone that I was... making love to a cantaloupe-headed sex mannequin made out of my grandma's old clothes, are you? Because that would be really uncool."

"I dunno," she said. She was trying to sound flirty but it came across more as threatening. "You know, I got in a lot of trouble for you, Trevor. My mother was not very happy that I drove her car into your house. And your parents didn't seem very happy either.

Buncha buzzkills. So I guess I can guarantee you my silence, but that all depends on what you're gonna do for me…"

"Oh man, you're not blackmailing me into going to prom with you, are you?"

She was just going to ask for a stick of gum, but now that he mentioned it, the prom thing was a waaaaaaay better idea.

"Yeah!" she said. "Yeah, that's exactly what I'm doing. I'm blackmailing you."

Trevor exhaled. He weighed his options. He had a reputation to maintain, and while he normally wouldn't be caught dead fraternizing with someone like Elizabeth Sturgis, he figured he'd be a lot worse off if all the dudes on the basketball team knew about Cummy Sue.

Cummy Sue was what he named his fuckdoll, by the way.

"Alright, even though I'd rather crap in a sock, then wear that sock, then eat that sock, then crap that crap-filled sock out and wear it again - if you keep your fat trap shut about Cummy Sue I'll…" he gulped. "…I'll go to the prom with you."

"ARE YOU FRIGGIN' SERIOUS RIGHT NOW???" she squealed.

"Um…yeah."

"The answer is yes, Trevor! Yes! Yes! 1000 times, yes!"

"Yeah whatever, just…chill the hell out, Lizardbutt before you pop a blood vessel or something. Just remember, it's *ix-nay* on the *exdoll-say*." He glanced down at the time on his phone. "Now if you'll excuse me I'm supposed to be fingering Annabel Lu in the backseat of my Audi in, like, 10 minutes. Hey, don't tell anyone about that either."

Elizabeth didn't hear that last thing he said because she had worked herself up into such a frenzy that she couldn't contain herself and threw up into her own hands. The picture she had drawn of Trevor came out in the regurgitated mess.

"I, um, I drew this for you..." she said as she handed him the vomit-caked paper.

CHAPTER THIRTEEN

"Bloodspilla! Bloodspilla! Hey, Elizabeth, wait up!"

Stevius called out to her from across the hall. She turned around and saw his horrible tiny plush body struggling to move as it hopped towards her. The squeaky pouch in his belly yipped with every step.

"HOLY FUCK! A TALKING DOLL!" she screamed as she kicked him. He slammed into a bank of lockers against the opposite wall, but got up almost immediately and dusted himself off. Apparently, toys didn't feel much pain.

"Elizabeth, it's me, your friend, Stevius. Remember?"

"Oh right. I forgot that you're the worst Satanist in history and turned yourself into a creepy living doll."

"Hey, I'm not creepy! I'm cuddly!"

"God, would you shut the hell up already so I can tell you something important?"

"What's going on?" he asked.

"Trevor Sandstone just asked me to the prom and I said YES!"

Stevius's face was blank. Partly because he was surprised and partly because it was difficult to emote with his plastic cheeks.

"No…way…" he said.

"Ew, don't sound so surprised, you vas deferens."

"What are vas deferens?"

"Who cares? Did you hear me? I'M GOING TO THE PROM WITH TREVOR FUCKING SANDSTONE!"

Elizabeth couldn't really tell for sure, but for a moment it sounded like Stevius was actually disappointed. But why would he be disappointed? She was about to get everything she ever wanted. He should be happy for her.

"Wait a minute," said Stevius, his cherubic face now lighting up. "If Trevor is going with you, that means Helena is free then, right?"

"OMG are you still gonna ask that slutzilla to go with you?"

"I am, unless you knew of anyone else who might want to go with me instead…"

"Maybe a Tickle Me Elmo?"

"So then yeah, I'm gonna ask Helena."

Elizabeth just shook her head. "Well I hope you enjoy getting chlamydia then because she's basically just a chlamydia vending machine."

Helena was putting her books away in a nearby locker, minding her own business.

"Just look at how slutty she's being!" Elizabeth said. "It's insane! She doesn't even know about how Trevor likes to finger Annabel Lu in the back of his Audi. Like, does she not have a sense of smell? What a slutzilla!"

"You're just a big hater, Elizabeth," Stevius said before taking a deep breath and casting his gaze determinedly at the popular girl. "Now wish me luck."

"Good luck DWEEBIUS," Elizabeth said. "You're certainly gonna need it."

Stevius squeaked his way across the hall.

"Um...Helena..." he apprehensively said.

"Oh aren't you just the CUTEST little dolly I've ever seen in my life!" she said, her voice pitched upward with delight. "You look just like the Baby Shits-Himself I used to have as a kid. Do you realistically shit yourself too, because that would be so CUTE!"

"I was actually wondering if you wanted to go to the prom with me."

"Look at you! Your stitches are coming out!"

Stevius spun his head around so that it was facing 180 degrees and he looked down at his bum. Sure enough, some of the stitching was coming out of one of his seams. Some cottony fluff was spilling through the opening.

"Oh jeez, this is really embarrassing. I swear, this never happens to me normally..."

"Nonsense. It's nothing to be embarrassed about. Lemme fix you up."

She pulled a stapler out of her locker and stapled him back together. Stevius involuntarily laughed, which is not a very goth-y response.

"Stop! Stop!" he chuckled. "That tickles!"

Helena put the stapler back and then squatted down so that she and Stevius were face-to-face.

"To answer your question: while I loved my Baby Shits-Himself growing up, I'm afraid I'm not going to be able to go to the prom with you. I have plans to go with my boyfriend, Trevor Sandstone."

"Actually, he's going with her..." He pointed to Elizabeth. "He asked her like 30 minutes ago."

"Um...what the hell *is* that thing?"

"Her names Elizabeth Sturgis," said Stevius. "She's a total slutzilla."

"Hey, I can hear you, you traitor jerk!" Elizabeth shouted to the two of them.

Helena was frowning now, her face scrunched up like a bulldog. She stomped over to Elizabeth and said, "What the heck is that little doll talking about? Why is my BOYFRIEND taking you to the prom?"

"Oh gee, I don't know, Helena. Maybe it's because he's tired dealing your worn-out front flap and he's looking to finally settle down with his ONE TRUE LOVE. He and I are destined to be together, FYI. We're like Romeo and freakin' Juliet in *Titanic*."

"I don't know what kinda game you're playing here, but I can assure you that Trevor is not tired of my worn-out front flap."

And once again, as if appearing on cue, Trevor entered the scene, approaching from the far end of the hall. Helena immediately stormed up to him.

"What is this I hear about you taking Elizabeth

Sturgis to the prom?" Helena asked her boyfriend.

"Huh?" he said. "Oh yeah. Yeah. Shit. I forgot about that. It's a long story, but basically, yeah, that's what's happening."

"Well were you planning on telling me???"

"Isn't that what I'm doing right now?"

"Ugh, you're just so selfish sometimes," she huffed.

"Look, I need you to calm your tits, babe. It's just a little bit of an extortion situation, but I got it all under control now. You're just gonna have to trust me okay?" He kissed Helena on the forehead. "Don't worry, you're still my number one, Helen."

"My name is Helena!"

"Yeah, that's what I said."

And he left.

"Just face it, Helena. You lost," Elizabeth said. "For the first time in your life, you lost and I won."

Helena glared at her. "You better believe I'm gonna get to the bottom of this. And if I have to get my uncle the SON of SAM involved you WON'T be very happy."

Emboldened, Elizabeth puffed out her chest and returned Helena's gaze with equal intensity. "You're uncle has been incarcerated for a very long time. He's no longer categorized as an active serial killer. He's just some old dude in some jail somewhere. My uncle, on the other hand, has his employee discount at Home Depot and has access to a LITERAL ARSENAL of chainsaws. He could max out his credit card and be ready to kill your whole family by the end of the afternoon."

Helena hadn't expected Elizabeth to stand up for herself, and she wasn't sure how to respond. "Hey Baby Shits-Himself?" she said out the corner of her mouth, keeping her unblinking eyes trained to Elizabeth's.

"What is it?" said Stevius, bouncing towards them until he was at Helena's side.

"On second thought, I think I will go to the prom with you."

She scooped him up in her arms.

"Really?" he said.

"Yeah. Really."

"This is pathetic," Elizabeth mumbled.

Stevius shot her admonishing look before turning his attention back to his hot new date. "Let's get out of here, Helena. This school suddenly feels SMALLER and STUPIDER than usual."

They turned and walked away from Elizabeth.

"Wanna go get a slice of pizza or something?" Helena asked him.

"I can't. I don't have a digestive tract anymore," Stevius replied.

"Oh, so you're NOT actually like Baby Shits-Himself then?"

"No, I guess not."

And then the two of them disappeared around the corner.

CHAPTER FOURTEEN

Trevor must've mentioned that he was taking Elizabeth to the prom to the freshly-fingered Annabel Lu while they were still in the backseat of his car because Annabel came up to her after the final bell rang for the day and said: "I heard Trevor is taking you to the prom."

Annabel's arms were crossed and her face was stoic, skeptical. Trevor Sandstone was going to the dance with Elizabeth Sturgis? This was an unexpected turn of events. Annabel wondered, was he in the middle of a stroke? Had he developed cataracts? Was he involved in some sorta *Freaky Friday* brain swap type scenario with someone hellbent on ruining his reputation? It was impossible to say for certain.

Annabel appraised Elizabeth like she would a rental car, eyes moving slowly from her head to her toes, noting all her flaws and imperfections as she went, perhaps looking for something that Trevor saw that she was currently missing. Inner beauty, or some stupid bullshit like that.

"Yeah he is," Elizabeth replied.

"Well, you're not a total lost cause, I suppose. I mean Trevor *must* have asked you for a reason right? Unless he's been replaced by a pod person and the alien now assuming his life is a masochist with a thing for uggos. But a quick trip to the salon to fix that rat's nest you call a haircut and a little make-up to cover up those acne crags, and I think we *might* be able to make you presentable."

"Thank you for believing in me," a sincere Elizabeth said to Annabel Lu, whom she now considered her new best friend.

"I don't believe in you, but we still got to try, don't we?" said Annabel. "Now c'mon. Let's go to the mall. It's time for the makeover sequence."

CHAPTER FIFTEEN

Elizabeth Sturgis sat in the passenger seat of Annabel Lu's Mercedes SLK trying (and failing) not to fart from excitement.

"Do you smell that?" asked Annabel Lu, her face scrunched up in repulsion.

"Yeah, I think you must've farted or something," said Elizabeth. "And honestly, I don't wanna sound judgmental Annabel, but you might want to get your butthole checked out by a butthole doctor because it smells worse than Mr. Belladonna's breath."

And then Elizabeth farted again because she was very eager to be seen out in public with one of the most popular girls in school and not feel like an uggo for once in her stupid pathetic life.

In fact, at that moment, Elizabeth felt like the opposite of an uggo. She felt like a secret princess who had finally been informed of her rite to the throne. First Trevor asked her to the prom, and then Annabel became her new bestie? This whole day was like something out of a fairy tale.

So her and Annabel filled the Mercedes with farts as the two of them sped down the suburban streets. During the trip, Elizabeth only expressed a single moment of doubt over the consequences of her current actions:

"Ya know, I'm actually grounded right now. My mom is being a real hard-ass lately. Not that I'm worried about getting caught. She's been picking up a buncha extra hours at work to pay off some outstanding house repairs she has, so she hasn't been around much. She's really bad at managing money apparently. All I'm saying is that I'm technically supposed to go home after school."

"Oh? And you do everything your momma tells you?" Annabel mocked her.

"Hell no!" Elizabeth said, trying to sound tough. "That would be super dorky if I did though, right? In fact, if you want to know, I NEVER do ANYTHING my mother tells me. One time my mother was like, 'Hey, could you help me bring these groceries in?' and I was all like 'How about YOU go eat the mummified turds out of a homeless guy's underwear, you saggy-boobed turd-eatin' bitch?'"

"Whoa, you actually said that to your mother?"

"You bet your perfectly-proportional ass I did. I'm basically an adult already, right? I'm 17.85 years old. I don't gotta answer to her or anybody else. I'm in charge of my own life."

They arrived at their destination and Annabel parked her car sideways in the handicap space.

"I'm allowed to do this, by the way. I'm dyslexic," she justified herself and the two of them went into the mall.

CHAPTER SIXTEEN

The two girls went to the nail place and got manicures. It was the first time Elizabeth had ever gotten a manicure. Once her nails were buffed, filed, painted, and lacquered, she looked at her hands like it was the first time she ever saw them, like she was a primate that just discovered she had opposable thumbs.

"I feel so fancy!" Elizabeth exclaimed. "I feel just like a *homo habilis!*" She gave the manicurist a thumb's up to show off her new thumb-bending abilities. The manicurist gave her a thumb's up in return. It was like they were in *Top Gun* or something. Elizabeth was Maverick. Annabel was Iceman. The manicurist was Goose. And Trevor was Kelly McGillis's character, whatever her name was.

And as pretty as Elizabeth Sturgis was feeling in that moment, she felt it doubly so by the time she and

Annabel left the hair salon. It took the stylist several hours and a half-dozen pairs of scissors, but eventually Elizabeth's hair was cut, washed, highlighted, and styled. Elizabeth was in awe of how much difference a little personal hygiene could make. Imagine what would happen if she brushed her teeth every once in a while? Crazy!

They sat on a bench and ate some pretzels from her favorite pretzel stand, Mr. Specialz Crusty Pretzels, and they drank big fountain sodas from her favorite soda stand, Mr. Spodaz Crusty Sodaz. Annabel pulled a make-up kit out of her purse and brushed some blush on Elizabeth's cheeks and put a bit of shadow on her eyes.

"I've never really worn make-up before," said Elizabeth, her mouth full of pretzel cud.

"Yes, I can tell. You don't really have the skin for it either. It's like throwing a cup of water into the Grand Canyon and calling it a river. But we're doing our best, right?"

Elizabeth looked at herself in Annabel's pocket mirror. She couldn't believe it. It was like she was wearing someone else's head. This must be how movie stars feel all the time. Like they're walking around with someone else's head on.

Lastly, the two of them went into Macy's to hit up the formal wear, stopping by the perfume counter along the way.

"Good call," Elizabeth said to Annabel, squirting a cloud of *Obsession* out of the tester bottle. "You can use the perfume to cover up all those farts you can't stop laying."

Elizabeth tried on so many dresses it was like she was some kind of dress-trying-on machine. She would come out of the dressing room to model each one for the discerning and perpetually critical glare of Annabel Lu.

"Too pink and too puffy," she said of a pink one with puffy sleeves.

-and-

"Too yellow," she said of a canary yellow one. "It's like you're wearing a puddle of human pee."

-and-

"You look like some kind of tropical fish," she said of another, a multicolored dress, covered in cheap plastic sequins. "You want Trevor to think he's slow-dancing with a giant tuna?"

"Are tunas colorful?" asked Elizabeth.

"How the hell should I know?" Annabel replied.

Elizabeth was exhausted. While she was enjoying herself, she had a brief moment where she stopped and wondered if this was really the best use of her time and energy. Did it actually take this much effort to be popular? The popular kids always made it appear so easy. Like they were born cool. Like they were a different species than her, better bred, generations of coolness distilled, progeny after progeny, until the modern day, the apex of eons of cool people selectively mating. But now she thought that maybe she had been mistaken. Perhaps *coolness* was just an illusion. A trick. A deception. And perhaps the coolest among us were secretly just as insecure as everyone else. Perhaps she had been chasing the wrong goals all along. Perhaps she would be better off trying to be true to herself instead of trying to appease a bunch of self-righteous assholes who never treated her nice in the first place. Good God, this felt like some kind of mental breakthrough, like some kind of personal revelation. It was almost as if she...

"THAT'S IT!" shouted Annabel, clapping her hands, derailing Elizabeth's entire train of thought. "That's the one."

Elizabeth was standing there in a wedding dress.

"Isn't this...a wedding gown?"

"It looks amazing," said Annabel Lu. "It's the most beautiful dress I've ever seen."

"Sure, it's nice and all, but is it really appropriate for a high school dance? Shouldn't I save this for mine and Trevor's inevitable wedding?"

"Look, beauty all about creating symmetry, about balance, right? So think of it this way: you're already butt ugly, so proportionally-speaking, the more beautiful your dress is, the closer to average you become."

"I'll admit I'm no Allen Einstein, but that math makes sense to me!"

"Of course it does," Annabel said as she stepped up behind her and the two of them gazed into the full body mirror. Annabel reached over and pulled down the veil so it obscured Elizabeth's face. "And look, another step closer to average as we speak!"

CHAPTER SEVENTEEN

Alright, enough beating around the bush. Time to get to the third act! Smash cut to the everybody-getting-ready-for-the-prom montage:

There was Trevor Sandstone, fresh out of the shower, shirtless, greasing up his perfectly coiffed hair. He slicked back the sides and combed up the front, styled it into a pompadour so ridiculously tall that it looked like a tidal wave roaring across his forehead. He put on his tailored tuxedo. Tied freshly-polished Oxford shoes. He looked at himself in the mirror, smiled, and almost ejaculated in his pants at the glorious sight of his own reflection.

There was Stephen 'Stevius Blaadfist' Finkelstein, waking up from a nap in his little sister's toy box. She must've mistaken him for one of her own dolls and stuck him in there when she was done playing. She had dressed him up like a pretty pretty princess, even brushed makeup on his plastic cheeks. He climbed out and searched all over her room for the Victorian crushed velvet suit and cape that he bought for the dance at Build-A-Bear, but he couldn't find it anywhere.

"Hannah!" he screamed. "Hannah, you dumb slut, where'd you put my clothes?"

"Awww, wittle pwincess don't wike her dwess?" his sister baby talked him.

"No, I don't like it. It's not even black," he said. "It's not goth at all."

There was Helena Berkowitz in her bathroom spraying the wet stank from her vagina all over the place like an angry skunk. Okay, okay, maybe that wasn't *actually* happening, but Elizabeth didn't give a fuck what that ho-bag was up to. Probably shaving her armpits or something like that.

There was Mr. Belladonna, already at the school. The final preparations for the dance were wrapping up before the students arrived. As the last decorations were hung, he discreetly poured a shot of 151 proof rum from a flask into his coffee mug and took a slow, satisfying sip. It was going to be a long night.

And, of course, there was the heroine of our story, Elizabeth Sturgis, who wasn't getting ready for the prom at all because her mother happened to have the evening off for some unknown and unjust reason. Seriously, why wasn't she at work? What were the chances? Didn't she owe money to people? What a lazy-ass!

So Elizabeth was pouting. Head buried beneath

her covers, eyes full of tears. She finally scored a date with Trevor, and now she wasn't allowed to go? This was some twisted M. Night Shyamalan style bullshit. Clearly, this was the most tragic moment in Elizabeth's teenage life, and in all honesty, it might have even been one of the most tragic moments in ALL of HUMAN HISTORY, depending on who you're asking. In Elizabeth's opinion, the list of mankind's most tragic moments went as thus:

1. The Toba Catastrophe (occurring approx. 75,000 years ago) wherein a supervolcano located at the site of what is now Lake Toba in Sumatra erupted. The ash and sulfur released during this cataclysmic event instigated a period of global cooling that lasted nearly 1000 years. This, in turn, caused the mass extinction of many plant and animal species, including significant portion of the human population, which dwindled down to an estimated 3000 to 10000 individuals (or between only 1000 to 5000 viable breeding pairs) a genetic bottleneck that completely changed the course of the planet's future evolution.
2. This night, right now.
3. I dunno, the friggin' Hindenburg Disaster or something.

The hottest piece of sausage in school had asked her out, and she was mentally and physically prepared to give him her first kiss that evening, in full view of God and her principal and Helena and everyone else who ever doubted her. And now her fartsucking mother had to screw the whole thing up?! It just wasn't fair!

Her mom tapped lightly on her door.

"Elizabeth?" she said through the thin wood.

"Go away!" cried Elizabeth, but her mom entered anyway.

"Hey honey, I thought you might be hungry so I brought you some soup."

"SOUP ISN'T FOOD, YOU HAG. IT'S JUST FLAVORED WATER. IT'S BASICALLY LIKE HAVING GATORADE FOR DINNER."

"Now honey, I don't want to have this debate with you again. Soup is food. There are vegetables and stuff in it."

"I don't understand any of this mom. I was asked by Trevor to the prom and yet, you are preventing me from going. It's the like universe is conspiring to keep me and my ONE TRUE LOVE apart."

"Trevor Sandstone? That handsome boy who's house you drove my car into?"

"It's called flirting, mom."

"He asked you to prom?"

"Is that so impossible to believe?!?"

"I not sure what kind of game he's playing, but I just need you to know I am doing this for your own good, Elizabeth. Boys like Trevor only want one thing."

"Yeah. My hot puss. I know mom. That's the whole fuckin' point."

"You're just too naive for this world, Lizzy."

"And you're too cynical," she said back.

Her mom considered this for a few seconds. Then signed.

"Perhaps one day we'll meet in the middle," she said,

her voice full of melancholy. She didn't like punishing her daughter, but she felt a responsibility as a parent to follow through. "I'm still your mother. And I'm still in charge. I'm sorry, sweetheart but that's the way it is."

And she got up and left, closing the door behind her.

Elizabeth wailed. She ran up to her bedroom window and looked outside and watched the everyone-else-getting-ready-for-the-prom montage happening all around her.

"Fuck this fucking bullshit," said Elizabeth, sniffling. "Nothing's gonna stop me from taking what's mine. Not even the Toba Catastrophe."

She turned around and opened her closet. She pulled out her wedding/prom dress and squeezed into it like toothpaste in a tube. She gave herself one last look in the mirror and nodded. So she was gonna sneak out. So what? What's the big friggin' deal? Is she gonna get grounded some more? Double grounded? There ain't no such thing. She'll be 18 in a month and a half and then she'll legally be allowed to do whatever she wanted, so what's a few more days punishment in the face of a lifetime's worth of memories?

She climbed out her bedroom window, shimmied across the eave, and dropped down into the side yard, all the while thinking: What's the worst that could possibly happen?

CHAPTER
EIGHTEEN

A black limousine rounded the corner down the street from Elizabeth's house.

She leaped out of the bushes in front of it, trying to get them to stop and pick her up. The driver slammed on the brakes but it was too late. Elizabeth bounced off the hood of the vehicle and went rolling across the pavement.

"What the hell was that?" asked Trevor from the backseat. He was in there with Darius Moore and Annabel Lu.

"I think we hit a whale or something?" said the driver.

"A whale? In the suburbs?"

"Well maybe it escaped from the aquarium. I don't know, bruh. I'm just a limo driver, not a fuckin' oceanographer."

Elizabeth shot up and pressed her body against the outside rear window of the car, face smushed against the glass, blood and mucus leaking from her nose, smearing everywhere. The three teenagers in the back screamed.

"Trevor?" she said. "Trevor is that you in there?"

Trevor opened the door, looked at her with confusion and disgust.

"Elizabeth? What the fuck are you doing? Didn't you message me an hour ago and tell me you weren't gonna make it out tonight?"

"Nope, you must have misread the text. You might be dyslexic like Annabel, I don't know. But I forgive you for not knowing how to read, my precious. What it actually said is I *AM* coming. And here I am! Ready for the prom! Everything is as it should be!"

More blood squirted from her clearly broken nose.

"Christ, get in here, hurry up, before the rest of your brain leaks out of your head," he said, pulling Elizabeth into the limousine by her arm.

She smiled. She was missing a few teeth.

"My chariot awaits!" she said, taking a seat next to Trevor.

CHAPTER NINETEEN

The limo pulled up in front of the school gym, which had been decorated with some balloons and streamers and a bunch of other shiny bullshit. It looked prom-y as fuck.

Trevor had purloined a single beer from his dad's refrigerator. The four teens shared it on the ride over.

"Underage drinking??!?" Elizabeth said in shock when Trevor pulled the can of room temperature Coors Light out of his jacket pocket. He cracked open the tab and slurped the first sip.

"You gonna narc on us?" asked Darius as he took a sip himself.

"No way, I'd never!" said Elizabeth. "In fact, I am totally into underage drinking. I do underage drinking all the time. It's my number one hobby. Lemme see that…"

Annabel took a small sip and passed it to Elizabeth who threw back her head and chugged the rest of the can.

"OH MY GOD I'M SO DRUNK RIGHT NOW!" she shouted into her prom date's face. "I FEEL MYSELF LOSING MY INHABITIONS, TREVOR, JUST IN CASE YOU WERE CURIOUS ABOUT WHERE MY INHABITIONS CURRENTLY WERE!"

Trevor chuckled uncomfortably.

And now that they arrived at the prom itself, the buzz from the half a beer was truly working its magic in Elizabeth's system, making the twinkling of the lights seem even twinklier, making the bouncy pop music sound even bouncier, making the smiling faces of her classmates and peers seem friendlier, even though almost all of them were eyeballing her with a WTF-is-she-doing-here-with-Trevor-Sandstone kind of look. But Elizabeth didn't care. She strutted out of the limo with confidence, like she was Lindsay fuckin' Lohan at the premiere of *Herbie: Fully Loaded*, the train of her wedding/prom dress trailing behind her like the paparazzi.

Inside the gym and it was even more decorated than the outside, even louder and more colorful. A DJ in the corner was playing a bunch of throwback 80s tunes like 'Rio' by Duran Duran and the theme song from *Dirty Dancing* (whoever it was that sung that, I don't remember) and everyone was dancing and drinking red punch from a big punchbowl and HOLY SHIT Elizabeth couldn't believe she almost missed out on what was already the best night of her entire life just because her mom was being an oppressive fartface.

And speaking of the oppressive fartface herself, back at the house, Elizabeth's mother had a moment of reflection and decided that maybe she was being a tad too harsh on her daughter, keeping her from the big dance, trying to force her to eat soup for dinner, et al. Elizabeth did make a valid point, her mother conceded. Soup kinda was just flavored water if you really thought about it.

She went up the stairs to apologize, to set things right, and fully explain herself.

knock knock

And when Elizabeth didn't respond, her mother spoke solemnly through the closed door:

"Elizabeth, it's your mom. I just wanted to say I am sorry for snapping at you earlier. It's just that there are things about yourself you do not know. Things about your biology that make you…different from the other girls. I know you've felt it, this fire inside you, burning bright and beautiful. But Elizabeth, that fire can also be dangerous if not handled properly. How can I explain this to you in a way that'll make you understand?"

Her mother exhaled. Continued.

"Back in the 80s, when I was a teenager myself, the world was a very different place. We were at the tail end of the Cold War and tensions with the USSR were still running high. I'm sure you've seen *Red Dawn*. Seems kinda outlandish in retrospect, but Soviet invasion was a legitimate existential threat back then. We were all scared of nuclear annihilation. We wanted to do everything we could to protect ourselves, our country, our way of life, so I…I…I let the US government install a missile silo inside of my vagina. I know it sounds crazy, but secrecy was our only advantage. Hide our weapons in a place no foreign government would think to look, armed and ready to launch should it come down to it. I was very patriotic in those days, a regular Betsy Ross, and so I volunteered my body for this experimental new procedure.

"I let them reconfigure my DNA, granting my uterus both the space and fortitude to house these foreign objects indefinitely. I was injected with a syringe full of shrunken down government workers. Tiny, brave men filled my body -engineers and scientists alike- working tirelessly inside me to defend the good ol' US of A.

"They put a missile inside of me, Elizabeth. A missile both big enough and powerful enough to cause unprecedented devastation. And what I'm saying is…I think I passed it down to you. That is why I am so strict sometimes. To keep you safe. Elizabeth, there's a very good chance that you've got a highly-volatile nuclear device in your vagina too, and until you learn proper breathing and Kegel techniques, any undo excitement could possibly set it off. That includes the mythological "first kiss" scenario that you've spent the past few years building up in your head.

"Honestly, I was hoping I would be able to spare us this conversation. That my missile would somehow skip a generation or something. But I was a fool. I know that now.

"Your body is a weapon, Elizabeth, and if you're not careful, you could end the world. I'm telling you, this could be worse than the Toba Catastrophe. You know about the Toba Catastrophe, right? That supervolcano that erupted 75,000 years ago at the site of what is now Lake Toba in Sumatra? Well, if you don't, lemme just say: it was bad. I'll send you a link to the Wikipedia article if you want to read up on it further.

"My point is: I'm sorry I didn't tell you any of these things earlier. I was hoping I wouldn't ever have to. I was hoping you'd remain my little girl forever. That you'd never grow up. But you're a woman now, Elizabeth. You deserve to be treated as such. And I want to tell you how to disarm the bomb before it's too late."

Elizabeth said nothing, because she wasn't home.

"Elizabeth, are you in there?" her mother said.

Still no answer. Obviously.

"Elizabeth?"

Her mother cracked open the door and peered inside. The room was empty. The curtains by the open window fluttered in the breeze.

"Shitballs!" she exclaimed as she ran down the stairs, grabbed her car keys off the key-holder-thingy by the front door, and headed out to the high school.

CHAPTER TWENTY

Elizabeth was on the dance floor, grinding on Trevor Sandstone while Trevor stood there and looked at his watch and yawned. It was like a dream come true.

"I'm backin' dat ass up, Trevor," she said. "I know you like it when girls back dat ass up."

"Whatever, just be careful that your bony butt cheeks don't cut me. Those things are like razor blades."

"Yeah, well if that's the case then you better call me The Delicatessen because I'm about to slice that ham of yours," Elizabeth Sturgis seductively said.

"What the fuck does that even mean, you weirdo?" Trevor replied.

"Ms. Sturgis," Mr. Belladonna called out from the side of the room. "Please dance appropriately."

Elizabeth begrudgingly turned around and tried to embrace Trevor in a more traditional way but he wiggled out of her grasp, saying, "I'm gonna go drink some punch so try not to asphyxiate everyone in the gym with your toxic queef cloud while I'm gone."

"I'll save you a spot on the dance floor," she said as she turned to the random kid next to her and shoved him. "HEY, THIS SPOT IS SAVED FOR TREVOR SO BACK THE FUCK OFF, YOU NERD."

Trevor wandered over to the shadowy part at the far end of the gym to join Darius and Annabel who were already huddled up together in secrecy. The three of them formed a kind of cool-kid cabal, speaking to each other in whispers beneath the din of the music, looking over their shoulders every few seconds to make sure they weren't being eavesdropped upon. They looked very suspicious, like they were going over the final details of some kind of nefarious plan they were about to hatch. Elizabeth was somewhat jealous she wasn't standing in the shadowy part of the gymnasium with them, presumably conspiring to bully some OTHER unsuspecting student, but whatever. She'll have plenty of time to concoct her own plans to bully kids with Trevor after they were married.

The double doors to the gym opened and in walked Stevius and Helena. Helena had on a really nice and tasteful dress, tangerine-colored and contoured perfectly to her slender frame without being inappropriate for her age. Objectively-speaking, she actually looked very pretty for once, which was a damn shame because she really was the biggest slutzilla in the known galaxy. That was a proven FACT.

Stevius also looked like a dapper little man in his stupid velvet Build-A-Bear tuxedo. Elizabeth was still annoyed at her friend for taking her sworn enemy to the prom, but she couldn't help but think back fondly, to a few days before, when Stevius was still a HUMAN teenager and he ALMOST-KINDA-SORTA ate out her asshole before Buzzkill Belladonna showed up and, predictably, killed their buzz.

Yeah, Stevius was kinda a dweebo, and he was about as goth as a unicorn egg, but he was also the only person who was nice to her back before she had any social clout. Before she was dating Trevor Sandstone, the hunkiest hunk in the whole damn school. Stevius was nice to her BEFORE she was cool.

Helena spotted Trevor, Darius, and Annabel in the corner of the room and immediately took off to join them as well. They opened their huddle just enough to allow her to wedge herself into it.

Elizabeth took this moment to approach the now-alone Stevius.

"Hey, Minion," she said with a conciliatory smile.

"Hey, Bloodspilla," he replied and he might have smiled back, but maybe not. Honestly, it was difficult to tell what expression his plastic face was trying to make.

"You look really nice," she said. "You and Helena make a *gag* cute couple."

"Yeah? You really think so? Because I think you look really nice too. Is that a wedding dress?"

"We're supposed to be in formal wear, aren't we?"

"It looks good on you. And your hair is done up

79

real nice. And you smell kinda like...onions and dirty socks? What the hell?"

"I ate a durian right before Trevor picked me up."

"It's really pungent. Like, I don't even have an olfactory system anymore and I can still smell it. I can't believe that Trevor doesn't mind making out with you with that diaper breath."

"We haven't actually kissed yet," she said. "I guess he's saving it for after the dance. He's classy like that. I'm sure he wants it to be as perfect as I do..."

She exhaled mournfully and they both lapsed into silence. The DJ flipped the track from some poppy radio trash to a love ballad. She looked around for Trevor but he and his crew were nowhere to be found. She turned back to Stevius.

"Care to dance?" she asked him.

"Yeah, sure," he replied.

She picked him up and held him in her arms like the Baby Shits-Himself doll that he was and the two of them slow danced together. And at first they didn't even talk, just enjoyed each other's embrace. And as the song played on, she could once again feel a flicker of warmth beginning to emanate from somewhere deep inside her, growing stronger and stronger with each passing second. The smell of petroleum. The rumble of a jet engine. Flushness across her skin. These hot flashes couldn't be chalked up to a simple pituitary issue. Hot air was escaping her body like central heat through a ventilation duct. The faint sound of honking alarms could be heard in the distance, coming at her in waves, as if echoing upwards from the bottom of an unexplored cave.

"I—wanted to apologize," she said to Stevius while the two of them spun around to the music.

"Really? I don't think I've ever heard you apologize for anything before."

"That's because I've never been wrong before. But I've been thinking about it, and I may have been unfair to you the other day. I got so wrapped up in my own bullshit, I ignored the obvious fact that you're probably the only person who has been there for me since the beginning."

"Oh, it's okay—" he started to say but she interrupted him.

"No, it's not. I acted like a spoiled little shit. I mean, yeah, me and Trevor are totally gonna go ALL THE WAY tonight, and then we're gonna go ALL THE WAY BACK, and if there's time we'll probably go A FEW DIFFERENT WAYS TOO but that doesn't give me the right to treat you like a dick just because you suck at occultism and turned yourself into a really freaky looking Chucky doll. And I understand why you wanted to go to the dance with Helena. She's very cool and very pretty and I was wrong to try and get in your way."

"That's the thing, Elizabeth. Yeah, Helena is totally popular, and totally hot, and I'm not even sure if I can produce semen in my current physical state, but if I'm able to, I'd totally want to unleash ROPES all up inside that FOR SURE. But, if I'm being completely honest with myself, you're the one I ACTUALLY wanted to go to prom with."

"Me? Why?"

"Because…well…I have a crush on you."

"You do?"

"Elizabeth, I've had a crush on you since the first moment I saw you."

"Oh my god. Stevius, how could I have been so blind?"

"I don't really know. I thought for sure it woulda been obvious to you when I was tonguing your turd cutter in the auditorium, but I suppose I needed to be a bit more direct. I guess that's the lesson I had to learn throughout all this: to not be so timid when pursuing the things I want."

Elizabeth smiled. "Wow. Look at the two of us, experiencing personal growth. I don't know about you, but I'd say we both just reached a point of emotional honesty within ourselves and with each other."

He nodded. "So what's left then?"

"For me?" she replied. "Just my first kiss with Trevor. The perfect end to the perfect day."

And at then her mother walked into the scene, ready to spoil all the fun.

CHAPTER
TWENTY-ONE

Elizabeth's mom stood there, framed by the gymnasium's double doors. She was in her regular street clothes so she looked really frumpy and out-of-place compared to all the other people in their formal dresses and suits.

Elizabeth clocked her immediately.

"Shitballs!" she said, as she dove with Stevius under a nearby table. The two of them curled up together like soldiers in a foxhole.

"What's going on?" asked Stevius.

"My fuckin' dumb frumpy mom is here."

"Is she a chaperone or something?"

"No, she's looking for me. I got grounded after I drove her car into Trevor's house, but I snuck out anyway. Like I was gonna miss the prom? Fat chance! She somehow figured out where I was like she's goddamn Sherlock goddamn Holmes or something."

Elizabeth's mom craned her neck and looked

around, trying to locate her daughter. When she couldn't find her, she went up to Mr. Belladonna.

"Hello, teacher-person? Hi. You're in charge, right? Maybe you can help me. I'm looking for someone. Elizabeth Sturgis. I'm her mother. Have you seen her here?"

"Yeah, I thought I did," Mr. Belladonna craned his neck to look around as well. "She was grinding very suggestively on Trevor Sandstone not too long ago. He's the captain of the basketball team, you know. He's really cool. I thought it was odd that they came here together. He's way out of her league. I can only assume there's some kind of blackmail afoot."

"That is SO like her," Elizabeth's mom shook her head. "I try my best to be a good mother, but she's a bit of a wild card. Ever since her father slipped on that banana peel and fell into the shark tank at SeaWorld, she's been acting out. I think she just lacks a positive male role model in her life."

"I'm sorry to hear about your husband," Mr. Belladonna sincerely said. "Honestly, I can relate. My late wife also slipped on a banana peel while we were at SeaWorld. She ended up falling into the penguin enclosure. They...tore her to pieces. I could only watch in horror as she was disemboweled and consumed by the vicious flock of flightless birds."

"I saw the footage of that on the news. It was both the cutest and saddest thing I'd ever seen."

Mr. Belladonna solemnly nodded.

The music stopped. Mr. Belladonna looked towards the small stage set up at the front of the room. "If you'll excuse me, Mrs. Sturgis, I have a few announcements that I have to make. Feel free to hang out. I'm sure Elizabeth will show up shortly."

He walked onto the stage and stood in front of the microphone. The music stopped and the student body gathered around.

"I hope you're all enjoying yourselves tonight," he said, voice booming through the PA. "I'm happy to report that horseplay has been kept to a minimum, and that general tomfoolery is currently at acceptable levels, so good job acting like mature adults everyone."

"SUCK IT, BELLADONNA," some jokester in the crowd yelled.

"Well great, now your tomfoolery quotient just went up by three points, so good job whoever said that. Anyway, before you all get back to dancing and having other forms of wholesome teenage fun, it is my distinct honor to present to you the most important moment of the whole night -perhaps the most important moment in your whole LIVES- the King and Queen of the Prom!"

A smattering of applause. A few hearty *whoop-whoops*.

"Can I get the envelope?" Mr. Belladonna said.

Annabel Lu skulked out of the shadows and handed him a sealed envelope. She smirked and slunk back away.

"Thank you, Ms. Lu." He turned to the DJ. "And can I get a drum roll please?"

"I...don't have a drum roll track," the DJ said.

"Well fuck," said Mr. Belladonna. "I guess we'll just

have to do this in total silence then. Weird. Anyway, without further ado, your Prom King and Queen are…" he pulled the names out of the envelope and read, "TREVOR SANDSTONE AND ELIZABETH STURG—Elizabeth Sturgis? Really? Are y'all serious? Wowwwww."

Everyone in the room started clapping harder now, like raindrops on a tin roof, deafening and torrential, for their new King and Queen.

Under the table, Elizabeth's eyes were shocked wide open.

"Did they just call my name?" she asked Stevius.

"They did!" he replied and he started clapping too.

"Oh my god, oh my god, I can't believe it!"

She poked her head over the edge of the table like a groundhog. The spotlight found her and the applause grew even louder. Elizabeth stood up. The smile on her face nearly swallowed her ears.

She looked over to her left and spotted her mom. She assumed she was going to stomp over and start yelling at her in front of everyone and embarrass her and ruin her life, but instead of her mom acting like the crusty old bi-otch that she normally was, she was cheering along for her daughter with the rest of the student body. They briefly made eye contact, and for the first time in her life, Elizabeth could sense the mutual respect flowing between them. Her mom was actually PROUD of her.

Everything seemed to be moving in slow motion. People parted, gave Elizabeth a clear path to the stage where Trevor was already standing, crown on his head.

As she walked up there, she received a few friendly pats on the back and a couple of hoots and hollers in support. Everyone was on her side.

To the right of the stage Helena, Darius, and Annabel stood. They were clapping too, but they were doing it in a much more foreboding way. Like they were clapping ironically because they were up to something sneaky. But never mind all that! This was THE BEST THING THAT HAD EVER HAPPENED TO ELIZABETH STURGIS SO SCREW THEM. Screw anyone who ever underestimated her. It was all so perfect that there was literally no way things could possibly go wrong so BANISH THAT THOUGHT from your mind, you cynical bastard. This was Elizabeth's time to shine!

She stuck her middle finger in Helena Berkowitz's face as she passed by her.

"Looks like you lose, you loser, so how about you go blow your serial killer uncle and then drown yourself in a hepatitis-filled toilet bowl!" Elizabeth said to her rival as she took her place on the stage next to Trevor. Elizabeth was not a very gracious winner, but she was a winner, nonetheless.

Mr. Belladonna gently put a tiara on her head. She was handed a bouquet of flowers. The lights twinkled. The music reached a crescendo.

"Trevor!" she said to her date, tears in her eyes. "Trevor, look! I did it. I'm Prom Queen! It's some kind of miracle!"

"Oh it's not a miracle," said Trevor. "Me and my crew totally rigged the vote."

"Wh—what?"

"Yeah, obviously we rigged this whole thing. Helena actually had the most votes, of course. In fact, you didn't even get a single one. But we threw all the real ballots away and replaced them with a buncha fake ballots so you'd be the Prom Queen."

"You did that…for me?" her smile wavering slightly now, unsure of where this was headed.

"Yeah."

"That's so NICE of you."

"Well, we were doing to be nice…" he said.

"Why *did* you do it then?"

And then Helena yanked on a string, causing a bucket of pig's blood up in the rafters to tip over, sending its gory contents pouring down all over Elizabeth's head.

CHAPTER
TWENTY-TWO

Splat

The blood that landed on her wasn't just pig's blood, though.

Elizabeth WISHED it was just pig's blood.

I mean, some of it was pig's blood, of course. To be honest, it wouldn't be a proper school dance WITHOUT pig blood being involved in some way, and Elizabeth went into the evening fully expecting something like this to happen. She was very familiar with *Carrie*. A little bit of pig's blood on the prom queen; we've seen it all before. But, unfortunately, this bucket had ALL TYPES of blood AND guts in it, and somehow there seemed to be no bottom to it. Literal gallons upon gallons of entrails fell on her. Elizabeth was covered in incarnadine slop: Ostrich intestines. Hippo brains. Even the parts of a bunch of endangered black rhino INCLUDING their buttholes, which had been pried free from the ends of their digestive tracts with care and immersed in the sludgy waterfall. That last one was the most embarrassing of all, by the way. Thousands of saucer-shaped endangered black rhino buttholes raining down on her from the ceiling like puckered hail.

Trevor and his crew had snuck into the zoo earlier in the day and spent a good part of the afternoon slaughtering a veritable Ark's worth of different animals, harvesting their innards and other assorted carrion with the expressed purpose of dumping it on Elizabeth in front of everyone. The goop soaked through her wedding dress, turning the fabric bright red, offal piled up all around her in fleshy mounds. There must have been 200 species represented here, all of them reduced to raw shredded meat.

The crowd fell silent as the last drops plopped onto her head.

Trevor, Helena, Annabel, and Darius were laughing their asses off. A few of the other students started to giggle too.

Elizabeth stood there like some kind of gory mannequin. In shock. Unable to process what just happened. Even Mr. Belladonna didn't know what to do, although he looked like he was trying to stifle a chuckle as well. More and more students started pointing at her and laughing, and soon, the room was cracking up like she was Paula friggin' Poundstone.

Fuck this, Elizabeth thought. If Trevor wanted to

play hardball, then the truce was off. She didn't owe him her loyalty or confidentiality. It was time for some mutually assured destruction. She grabbed the microphone and said:

"I MAY LOOK LIKE AND IDIOT COVERED IN THE BLOOD OF ALL THESE DIFFERENT EXOTIC ANIMALS, BUT I JUST WANT YOU ALL TO KNOW TREVOR SANDSTONE MAKES LOVE TO A CANTALOPE IN A DRESS THAT HE CALLS CUMMY SUE! THAT'S RIGHT, HE'S A PERV. SO PLEASE REDIRECT YOUR RIDICULE IN HIS DIRECTION INSTEAD OF MINE, THANK YOU."

She smiled smugly at Trevor, but Trevor just smirked back at her.

"You dummy," he said. "They all know about Cummy Sue. Everyone in school already knows about Cummy Sue. I'm not ashamed of my fetishes. Nobody should be, as long as they are indulged in a safe and consensual way. For the record, it's not cool to kink shame people, Elizabeth." He turned from her and spoke into the microphone, addressing the rest of the crowd. "In fact, how many of you out there subscribe to mine and Cummy Sue's OnlyFans account?"

Literally everyone in the room raised their hand, including Helena, Stevius, Mr. Belladonna, and even her mother.

"Mom, seriously?" said Elizabeth.

Her mother just shrugged. "What? I think it's kinda hot. Contrary to how pop culture likes to portray women of a certain age, I haven't ceased being a sexual being just because I'm over 40. Please respect the fact that I gotta get my nut off too sometimes." She winked at Mr. Belladonna.

"Oh man, this was the greatest prank of all-time!" Trevor was laughing so hard now that tears were running down the corners of his eyes. "You are covered so much blood and you look so dumb. You're gonna have the Conservation Society all OVER your ass too. There are only like 4 of those black rhinos left now."

Elizabeth was a ball of fury. Her fists were clenched. Her brow was furrowed. She faced the rest of the class with scorn. She knew that hidden inside her was some kind of power. All her life she felt different, like a weapon without a launch code, like a bomb without a fuse. But today was supposed to be different. Today was supposed to change all that. And so she focused all her mental energy outward, ready to unleash hell on those who betrayed her. She imagined the doors to the gyms slamming shut and locking. She imagined a fire tearing through the building, setting this whole place ablaze with everyone still trapped inside.

"Oh shit! Everyone look out! She's gonna CARRIE us!" a random student cried out.

There was a brief moment of panic among the crowd, but that quickly passed as soon as everyone in the room realized Elizabeth didn't have any telekinetic powers and she wouldn't be able to Carrie anyone. All she did was shake in place for a few seconds before releasing a rage-fart that lasted for three solid minutes.

It was a real squeaker too, high-pitched, like a pinched balloon slowly letting out air.

Everyone burst out laughing again, this time so hard that one kid with a heart condition actually did die, so I guess she kinda Carrie'd him by accident, but honestly, if she had a revenge list the Heart Condition Kid would've been like 60th on it so there wasn't much satisfaction in watching him suffer.

Elizabeth ran from the stage.

She ran out of the school.

She ran down the street, heels going *clack-clack* on the pavement.

Ran past the edge of town.

Ran until the road ended and there was nowhere else left for her to go.

And she found herself alone, on an abandoned beach, at night, only darkness ahead of her, and the endless ocean.

CHAPTER
TWENTY-THREE

The moon shone down on her like a…moon-shaped thing.

"Fuck you, moon," she said to it while crying.

She buried her feet in the sand. She wished she could bury her whole body in the sand. She wished she could feed herself to crabs, let them pick her bones clean, leave her half-digested corpse at the bottom of the brackish sea along with the rest garbage dumped out by local fishing trawlers. There was no way even the most gnarly crab was as mean or as cruel as the kids in her school. She was born the wrong species. Life was not fair.

And then she heard a squeaking sound coming up from behind her, like a clown horn.

She turned and saw Stevius, slowly approaching.

"What do you want?" she sniffled. "Can't you see I'm in the middle of having a DARK NIGHT OF THE SOUL?"

"I wanted to check on you," he said. "And I wanted to tell you that I only subscribed to Trevor's OnlyFans because everyone else did and I didn't want to be left out. If it means anything to you, I never wanked off to it. Not even one time."

"I really thought I'd be able to Carrie them. I thought things were gonna go my way for once. I mean, I'm the HERO of the story, aren't I? That means I'm supposed to win at the end! If that's not how real-life works, then what good are movies anyway? They're lies! They're fake! All those John Hughes films are utter bullshit. Is he still alive? We should track him down and castrate him."

"Life doesn't always play by the rules, Elizabeth, but I still don't think your expectations were unreasonable," said Stevius.

"You don't?"

"No. You do deserve to be happy, just like everyone else. I just think you've been trying to find your answers in all the wrong places."

"What do you mean?" she said.

"Well...take a look around you. Here we are. On a beach. It's after prom. The moon is out..." He held out a single rose that he salvaged from the ground after Elizabeth tossed her bouquet away "...and I got this for you."

She took the rose from his tiny plastic hand and used it to wipe the boogers from her nose. She forced herself to smile at her one and only friend.

They looked out over the water.

"It's true," she said. "This is almost like I pictured it."

"What's missing?" he asked.

"The kiss."

He put his hand on her thigh and his gaze met hers.

"You know, I've never kissed anyone either…" he said.

"Stevius? What are you suggesting? That YOU were my ONE TRUE LOVE this whole time?"

"Well, duh. Did you really not see this coming? I thought you said you watched a lot of movies? Doesn't the best friend character get the girl at the end sometimes too?"

"Occasionally. Not in *Pretty in Pink* though."

"Yo, fuck that movie," he said. "She shoulda ended up with Duckie and everyone knows it. This is probably more like a will-they/won't-they *When Harry Met Sally…* situation."

"I guess I see where you're coming from," she said. "But that's not really a 'teen' movie."

"You're basically an adult now yourself, Elizabeth. Maybe it's time for your tastes in rom-coms to evolve too."

"So you want to kiss me then?" she asked.

"If you'd have me, of course I would…"

"Yes!" she enthusiastically consented. "NOW LET'S PLAY SOME TONSIL HOCKEY, YOU FREAKY LITTLE RAGGEDY ANDY-LOOKING MOTHERFUCKER!"

CHAPTER
TWENTY-FOUR

Their kiss was MAGICAL! Holy shitballs! It was better than she ever imagined it could be. It was world-changing. Earth-shaking. It was TRANSCENDENT!

Kissing Stevius was better than blackmailing Trevor into asking her to the dance. It was better than the false sense of 'acceptance' she felt when dress shopping with Annabel Lu. It was even better than the nine seconds she was the legit Prom Queen before the butchered menagerie was dumped onto her head. Her whole crappy life had been leading up to this moment, when her chapped and pimple-covered lips finally pressed against the cheap plastic lips of Stevius Blaadfist - her actual, factual ONE TRUE LOVE.

And then, the countdown inside of her began once again, but this time in earnest. She could feel it, like a tidal wave. Unstoppable. There was no turning back now. Her desire was absolute. She was a woman. She was ready to blow.

"*Launch sequence initiated. T-minus 10 seconds to ignition...*" the computerized voice inside her abdomen said.

Still their mouths were pressed against one another.

"*9 seconds...8 seconds...7 seconds...*"

Her belly mound swelled up and glowed orange. Noxious plumes of gray smoke poured out of her groin. They ignored it and continued kissing.

"*...6 seconds...5 seconds...4 seconds...*"

The muffled sound of men talking could be heard, tiny voices coming through of her skin like sweat. These were Oppenheimers of Elizabeth's peculiar chastity belt; the government men and technicians stationed inside her, the ones who maintained the bomb between her thighs for her entire life. You could hear them running along metal catwalks, screaming to take cover, scrambling to the safety of a fortified bunker hidden somewhere even further inside of her body.

"*...3 seconds...2 seconds...*"

Alarms were going off, so loud now that the two teenagers sucking face on the beach could only hear one another by speaking directly into the other's mouth:

"I love you, Elizabeth Sturgis," Stevius shouted into Elizabeth's open gullet.

"I love you too, Stephen Stevius Blaadfist Finkelstein," she shouted back into his.

The smoke was so thick they could barely see, barely breathe.

"*...1 second...*"

—and then—

"LADIES AND GENTLEMEN, WE HAVE LIFT-OFF!"

She was tossed backward a few feet, eyes wide in surprise. She spread open her legs like she was giving birth, hyperventilating through her teeth, white knuckles clutching handfuls of sand. Stevius looked concerned, and like the Baby Shits-Himself doll he somewhat resembled, an *oopsy* filled up his tiny trousers. Turns out he could poop himself after all.

"Is this supposed to be happening?" he crowed, hopping over so that he was standing next to Elizabeth's right shoulder, taking the position a proud father in the delivery room might take.

"I think I'm having some kind of SEXUAL AWAKENING or something!" she screamed, her voice barely audible over the roar of the gigantic nuclear missile that was now breaching her…ummm…what did Mr. Belladonna call that thing down there again? Her *lay-be-ya majora*? Ugh, could they make it sound any more gross?

"Something is coming…out of my…fucking… *CUP…CAKE…..*!" she sputtered, trying to retain whatever modesty she had left.

The missile pushed itself forward. Slowly at first. Just the cone at the top of the device, appearing in a cloud of exhaust like the roof of a steeple piercing a low-hanging fog. Elizabeth was stretched out in ways that should have split her in half, and yet, her body accommodated the bulk of the thing like it had always been designed for this task.

She clenched her jaw, pushed harder, so hard she almost fainted from the pain, the rest of the explosive passing through her, inch by agonizing inch, until the thing was completely born: a missile the size of a private jet, the emblem of the American flag emblazoned on the side, proclaiming it the property of the USA. Sand whipped all around them as it tilted itself upwards.

Inside her head she could hear the men clapping and cheering and slapping high-five, congratulating each other on a successful mission.

"We did it boys!" one of them said from inside her womb. Probably the commander. There was another round of raucous cheers and Elizabeth swore to herself that if she survived this horrible process, she would douche these miniature men out of her body and stomp on them into oblivion like ants they were.

She shimmied back a few feet and stood up. Stevius climbed up onto her back, peeked over her shoulder, shook his head in disbelief.

"This is crazy! You're a goddamn nuclear silo, Elizabeth! What are we supposed to do now? Raise this thing like it was our child?" he said into her ear.

"We've got to hop on!" said Elizabeth. "Before it takes off!"

"Hop onto the bomb? And then what? Ride it straight to hell?"

"I don't know, Stevius, but we need to see where it takes us. It's the only way!"

Elizabeth awkwardly straddled the missile. The shell of it was still covered in a layer of her gooey postnatal pee cream, but the heat of the engine was evaporating it fast. It stank like hell, but it also made it decidedly less slippery.

It took some effort to find purchase, but she was able to brace her feet against two large rivets and hold on with one hand to a random handle that seemed to have been placed there specifically for that purpose.

The thrusters kicked into high gear. The missile blasted off, into the sky, with the two of them clamped tightly onto the outside of it.

"Hey, we're like Slim Pickens at the end of *Dr. Strangelove*," said Stevius. "Ever see that one?"

"No, and nobody understands the reference either," said Elizabeth. "It came out in the 60s. That shit is for OLD people."

"Oh it's a cool movie, a Stanley Kubrick directed Cold War comedy that lampoons both the callousness of first-world leadership and the ineptitude of the military-industrial complex. You should check it out, Elizabeth. It's well worth your time."

"This seems like a somewhat unimportant topic of discussion considering our current predicament."

"Yeah, you're probably right," he said. "So are we going to die or what?"

"I honestly have no idea. I stopped paying attention in health class months ago," she replied.

"Yeah, me too. Mr. Belladonna was always boring as SHIT up there. What kind of grown adult wants to talk to teenagers about sex anyway? Dude's a straight-up molester."

"That's what I said!"

The missile roared above the ocean, traveling several 1000 miles per hour. The centrifugal force of it pushed Elizabeth's face back so that it didn't look like her normal busted-ass ugly-ass mug. Instead, it made her face look shiny and smooth, like she was a toy doll too, just like Stevius.

"You look beautiful," he said to her.

"I do?"

"Elizabeth, you're the most beautiful girl I've ever seen," he said.

The rocket traveled eastward, across the Atlantic, kicking up massive waves in its wake. Tsunamis were cast in every direction, crashing down upon unsuspecting costal shores. People sleeping in their homes in Africa and Europe and North and South America -from all the way from British Columbia to the tip of Argentina- were drowned in the sudden flood.

The missile continued forward still. Over the Middle East. Over Asia. People looked up and saw the nuclear device passing above them in all its terrifying glory. A contrail of gray smoke bisected the Heavens. The roar of it was unholy. The sound barrier was shattered. It was so loud it crumbled buildings and deafened children. But it traveled on.

Elizabeth and Stevius circled the globe on this thing, the two of them totally and irrevocably in love, Frenching hardcore the entire time. At one point Stevius even touched her boob a little bit and HOLY SHIT, it was so SENSUAL! Not only is she kissing a boy, but she also got to 2nd base!? This was the SINGLE GREATEST THING THAT HAD EVER HAPPENED IN ALL OF HUMAN HISTORY and it was happening to Elizabeth Sturgis like she always hoped and dreamed it would.

Over the Pacific, the bomb traveled. Back into America. Over California. Over all those flat boring states in the middle of the country that nobody ever remembers the names of. Wyoming? Is that even a real place? Ha ha. What kind of idiot would live there?

And then, on the horizon it appeared before them, like an oasis in the desert. Their target. Their purpose. Their final destination:

The high school prom that Elizabeth had just been ridiculed out of.

The entire student body walked out of the gym and gathered in the parking lot to see what all the commotion was about. Trevor and Helena. Darius and Annabel Lu. Even her mother and Mr. Belladonna too. Anyone that Elizabeth had ever known or interacted with, staring up at the missile aimed directly at them, tearing the stratosphere asunder, and coming in fast.

One by one, the people who had stood in opposition to her throughout her life -the bullies and naysayers and folks who tried to keep her down, the people like me and you who so callously laughed at Elizabeth's misfortune and pain- were forced to confront the absolute certainty of their own human frailty, and their inescapable doom.

And as the bomb fell to Earth, Elizabeth thought

of the movies she grew up watching, how they had impacted her perception of reality, how they had burdened her with these impossible expectations, and how unrealistic they all turned out to be. Ultimately, she had to follow her own path, as strange as it may have been. She could only be true to herself, and to her heart.

"Good lord, the tomfoolery quotient on this is OFF THE CHARTS!" Mr. Belladona said in terror as the missile crashed into the ground in front of them and detonated.

A fire roared across the globe, incinerating everyone and everything in its path. This was WORSE than the Hindenburg Disaster. Worse than the Toba Catastrophe, even. It was the Apocalypse, the End of Everything. Elizabeth Sturgis finally got her first kiss as the entirety of civilization was erased in a glorious flash.

Don't you just love it when the underdog wins?